## WE CAN READ!™

# Critter Day

by Jacqueline Sweeney

*photography by* G. K. & Vikki Hart
*photo illustration by* Blind Mice Studio

**B**ENCHMARK **B**OOKS

MARSHALL CAVENDISH
NEW YORK

*For G. K. and Vikki, Mark and Kendra,
who share the Critter dream*

*With special thanks to Daria Murphy, reading specialist
and principal of Scotchtown Elementary, Goshen, New York,
for reading this manuscript with care and for writing the
"We Can Read and Learn" activity guide.*

Benchmark Books
Marshall Cavendish Corporation
99 White Plains Road
Tarrytown, New York 10591

Library of Congress Cataloging-in-Publication Data
Sweeney, Jacqueline.
Critter day / Jacqueline Sweeney.
p.   cm. — (We can read!)
Summary: All the critters get ready for a day of games, including pond races,
leaf slides, and a pine climb.
ISBN 0-7614-1119-4
[1. Animals—Fiction. 2. Games—Fiction.]
I. Title II. Series: We can read! (Benchmark Books/Marshall Cavendish)
PZ7.S974255Cr   2001      [E]—dc21        00-024175 CIP          AC

Printed in Italy

1 3 5 6 4 2

# Characters

Ladybug

Molly

Jim

Eddie

Ron

Tim

Hildy

Big Owl

Gus

Ladybug sat on a maple leaf.
"Too big," she said.

Molly sat on a holly leaf.
"Too small," she said,
"and too sharp."

"What are they doing?" asked Eddie.

"Getting ready," croaked Ron.

"Sunday is Critter Day.

The owls are in charge."

"Games!" squealed Tim.

"Pond Race is for me," quacked Hildy.

"Watch me win!"

At last it was Sunday.

The owls had gray whistles.

Big Owl wore a brown hat.

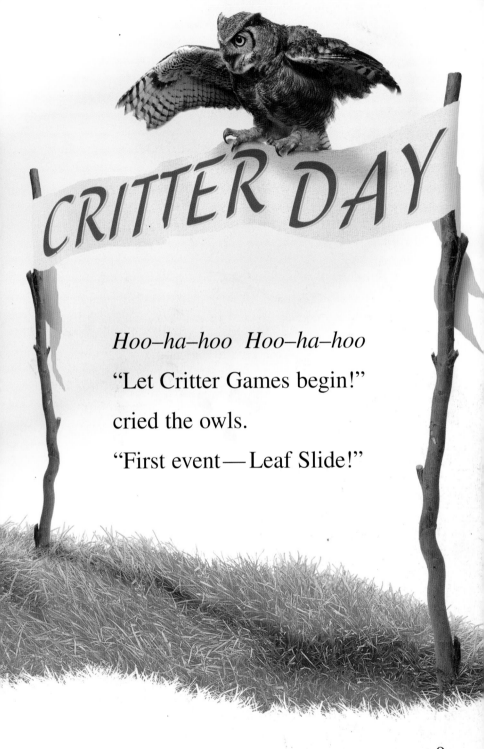

*Hoo–ha–hoo  Hoo–ha–hoo*

"Let Critter Games begin!"

cried the owls.

"First event—Leaf Slide!"

Molly chose first.

"I want the beech leaf," she squeaked.

"Willow," said Ladybug.

"Oak," croaked Ron.

"*Tweet!*" went Big Owl.

Down they slid.

Ladybug fluttered and fluttered

and won!

"Next event—Apple Roll!"

Hildy rolled her apple.

It rolled beside the hole.

Jim rolled his apple.

It stopped before the hole.

But Ron rolled his apple right in!

Pine Climb was next.

Eddie was ready. So was Jim.

Big Owl pointed up.

"Get that feather!" he said.

Up climbed Eddie.

Up climbed Jim.

They reached the feather together!

Berry Teams was next.

"Find your partner," hooed Big Owl.

"Go pick berries!"

They picked and picked
and ate and ate.

All except Gus and Molly—
they picked the most!

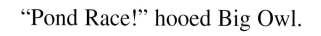

"Pond Race!" hooed Big Owl.

"Go under the branches,

over the log,

around Pond Rock,

and through the bog."

*Tweeeet!* The friends rowed.
They paddled. They splashed.
They fell in!

All except Hildy—she flew!

"Homemade Hats!" hooed Big Owl.

He pointed to six baskets.

"Use these," he said.

Molly chose berries.

Hildy chose reeds.

Eddie chose pinecones.

And Tim chose *everything*.

That night
the owls made a fire.

*Hoo–ha–hoo  Hoo–ha–hoo*
"Critter Feast!" they cried.
The friends began to eat.

*Tweet! Tweet!*
"Awards!" hooed Big Owl.

"Who won?" whispered Eddie.

"We all did," said Jim.

"All of us?" squeaked Molly.

"Of course," fluttered Ladybug.
"We're all good at something!"
Then Hildy sang the Critter Song.
And everyone joined in.

# WE CAN READ AND LEARN

The following activities are designed to enhance literacy development. *Critter Day* can help children to build skills in vocabulary, phonics, and creative writing; to explore self-awareness; and to make connections between literature and other subject areas such as science and math.

## CRITTER CHALLENGE WORDS

There are many challenging words in this story. After discussing the words in the list below, ask children to write them on index cards. Have a vocabulary race. Place the cards in two piles. Have two children stand at an equal distance from the piles. They race to pick up a word, use it in a sentence, and return to the finish line. Create a relay race by forming teams. Each member races to a card, uses a word in a sentence, and then selects a new card to hand to the next player.

| | | | |
|---|---|---|---|
| awards | climbed | critter | feast |
| feather | holly | paddled | partner |
| reached | row | sharp | together |
| whispered | whistles | | |

## FUN WITH PHONICS

The characters in this story created homemade hats from materials found in nature. Children can design and decorate their own hats, using paper as a base and adding materials found outdoors, in the classroom, or at home. Make sure children leave room on their hats to write one of the words below. You might give awards for the silliest hat, the scariest, the most beautiful, etc.

**Long a words:**

| | | | |
|---|---|---|---|
| Ladybug | homemade | games | race |
| gray | Sunday | day | ate |

**Long i words:**

| | | | |
|---|---|---|---|
| slide | pine | climb | night |
| cried | beside | right | fire |

## CREATIVE WRITING

The Critter Day events were great fun and very creative. Invite children to use their imaginations. Label paper lunch bags with the words "descriptions," "colors," and "days of the week." On index cards or small slips of paper, write words from each of these categories and place them in corresponding bags. (Add your own words to those listed below.) Children can choose one word from each bag to use as story starters. Create a new Critter Day event! Have children write and illustrate their own story.

**Descriptions:** big  small  sharp  good

**Colors:** gray  orange

**Days of the week:** Sunday  Monday  Tuesday

## POND RACES

Children can make their own pond races. No water is necessary! The animals in this story needed to know which direction to follow to complete the race. Write the words listed below on small pieces of paper. Set up an obstacle course using objects such as chairs, small tables, and blocks. The coach uses the words with the objects to give the racers their instructions. For example, "Go around the chair, under the desk, through the door, and over the blocks."

**Direction Words:**

| on | up | down | in |
|---|---|---|---|
| over | beside | next to | under |
| around | through | | |

## LEAF SLIDE SCRAPBOOKS

Each animal in the story chose a leaf for the leaf slide, such as beech, willow, or oak. Have children become leaf experts. Start by having them collect leaf samples, placing each one in a small plastic sandwich bag. Go to the library to research their collections. Label the leaves and tape or staple the bags together along one side to create leaf scrapbooks.

## AWARD WINNERS

Ladybug knew that each of us is good at something. Children can create original awards that celebrate what they are good at. They can make them for each other and for friends and family members too. Have fun making the awards with all kinds of materials. Children can recognize their own success and honor each other at a special awards ceremony.

## About the author

Jacqueline Sweeney is a poet and children's author. She has worked with children and teachers for over twenty-five years implementing writing workshops in schools throughout the United States. She specializes in motivating reluctant writers and shares her creative teaching methods in numerous professional books for teachers. She lives in Stone Ridge, New York.

## About the photo illustrations

The photo illustrations are the collaborative effort of photographers G. K. and Vikki Hart and Blind Mice Studio. Following Mark Empey's sketched storyboard, G. K. and Vikki Hart photograph each animal and element individually. The images are then scanned and manipulated, pixel by pixel, by Mark and Kendra Empey at Blind Mice Studio.

Each charming illustration may contain from 15 to 30 individual photographs.

All the animals that appear in this book were handled with love. They have been returned to or adopted by loving homes.

32